Teen Fiction:

A WORLD
OF
MY OWN

A Short Story Fantasy for All Ages

Teen Fiction: A World of My Own -
A Short Story Fantasy for All Ages
by Becca Bates
Published by Indie Artist Press
Eagle Mountain, Utah
www.indieartistpress.com
First Edition
ISBN 978-1-62522-063-9
copyright © 2015 Becca Bates
All rights reserved.
October 2015

ℙublisher's 𝔑ote

Thanks for taking the time to enjoy *A World of My Own* by debut author Becca Bates. We know you'll enjoy this journey as much as we did.

To thank you for your purchase, we invite you to visit Becca's website at

http://beccabates.weebly.com

where you'll find a gift from the author: another short story, free to those who sign up for her newsletter mailing list.

Thank you again for reading
A World of My Own,
and happy reading.

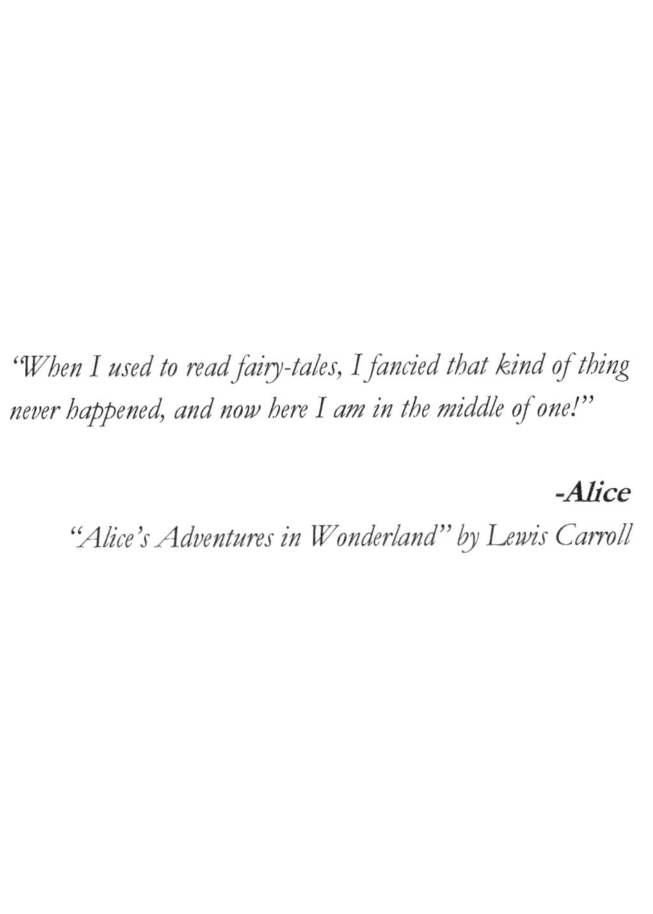

"When I used to read fairy-tales, I fancied that kind of thing never happened, and now here I am in the middle of one!"

-Alice

"Alice's Adventures in Wonderland" by Lewis Carroll

A World of My Own

The alarm yanks me from my dream. I groan and grasp for any remainder of the dream, but already it fades from my mind. It was a good one, too. My dreams are usually a welcome escape, but then morning comes along and steals the ending.

I take a deep breath and plunge into my completely predictable day. After changing and brushing my teeth, I head to the kitchen where my mother sits staring at a wall. That's all she ever seems to do anymore. She resurfaces every now and then, but I've learned to stop expecting it by now. She has a wonderful smile, though you would never know. It must have been almost a decade since I last saw it. I throw a handful of strawberries on a small plate and pour myself a bowl of cereal, and another one for Lily, who bounces through the door. My little sister is the only source of energy in the entire house, and the only thing I like about it.

"Marie," she says, whining the way that so many six-year-olds do. "I'm tired of cereal."

"Too bad. If you don't want it, you could always have strawberries."

"Blech," Lily says, scrunching her nose in disgust like I knew she would. "I hate strawberries."

"Cereal it is. Now hurry up or we'll be late again."

I suppose it's my fault we're always late. I tend to set the alarm as late as possible. Lily sticks her tongue out at me, but soon breaks into a giggle.

"What's so funny?" Lily's father, Hank, growls as he joins us in the kitchen, quieting Lily's laugh. He grabs the bottle of aspirin from the shelf and pours a couple of tablets into his palm before popping them into his mouth and swallowing them with a swig of orange juice from the carton. I honestly don't know how he manages to go to work with a massive hangover every single day and not get fired. Lily and I eat in silence as he rips open a granola bar and stomps out the door. I let out a breath of relief that he's gone so easily this morning. I really didn't want to deal with him today.

"Come on," I tell Lily when we finish our food. "Let's go."

We put our bowls in the sink and Lily gives Mom a kiss on the cheek, smoothing her untidy hair before we head out the front door. Mom, as always, doesn't react.

Lily grabs my hand as we walk down the sidewalk to her elementary school.

"Do you get the costumes today?" she asks. A hint of a smile escapes before I can stop it. I'd forgotten that was today. Of course, that also means the one thing that brightens my day will be ending soon, but I'll deal with that when it comes.

"Yes."

"I can't wait to see you all dressed up tonight," Lily says.

"I can't bring it home," I say, rolling my eyes. "You'll have to wait until tomorrow, just like everybody else."

"Aw," Lily makes a sad, puppy-dog-face.

"I don't make the rules," I say. I wish I did. Things would be very different.

~*~

My day at school passes by in a blur. I spend most of my classes drawing pictures of the Cheshire Cat at various stages of visibility in the margins of my notes. During lunch, I sit alone at a corner table and observe the teeming crowds of high schoolers as they head to their usual tables and jabber with their friends. No one even tries to join me. Yes, it becomes lonely at times, but I'd rather be alone than fake my way through pleasantries.

By last period, I'm itching for the bell to ring. The best part of my day is on its way, and today will be even better. As soon as Algebra ends, I push my way through the students crowding the halls to the auditorium. Mikayla stands by a rolling clothes rack and a large plastic tub, both of which are packed with clothes and accessories. She smiles at me as I beeline for her.

"Hey, Marie," she says, pulling a dress off the rack. "I finished it this morning."

"Thank you," I say, taking it from her, "it's perfect!"

A white apron covers the front of the blue dress. White stockings are draped around the top, and a black ribbon is tied to the hanger.

"Don't forget the shoes," Mikayla says, handing me the black flats.

I race to the dressing room and change. I look at my reflection in the full-length mirror. I had tried it on once before, for the fitting, but the dress had been too big at the time. Now I can't help but smile as

I see Alice reflected back at me.

Acting has always been my favorite hobby. The chance to become someone else and live in their world for a while is almost as good an escape as dreams. This year has been exceptionally good because the school chose to produce a play based on Alice in Wonderland, one of my all-time favorite stories, and I managed to land the lead role. On top of that, I get to share a few scenes with Leo Hughes, the love of my life.

Leo moved across the street from me two years ago from Oxford, England. As if being British wasn't awesome enough, he also came from the very city in which *Alice's Adventures in Wonderland* was first conceived. He's even been to the real Old Sheep Shop. Rehearsals are the only time I talk to him. I can never quite work up the nerve outside of drama club. It's a shame that after this week I'll no longer have an excuse for to do so.

~*~

hey gave it to me," Leo says, "for an un-birthday present."

"I beg your pardon?" I ask.

"I'm not offended," Leo says.

"I mean, what *is* an un-birthday present?"

We're about three-quarters through the dress rehearsal and I have to admit, Leo looks rather absurd in his Humpty Dumpty costume. Somehow he still manages to be adorable.

"A present given when —"

A few screams of surprise echo through the auditorium as the sprinklers go off and a loud bell threatens to deafen us. Around us, the room descends into complete chaos as the cast and crew flee from the unexpected deluge and out the fire exits. The stage director bumps into my arm as he passes with a clipboard over his head like an umbrella.

Leo hops down from the stand disguised as Humpty's brick wall. He can't move well in the costume and tumbles to the ground. I offer him my hand and help him off the stage. We're soaked through by the time we make it outside, and from the look of the darkening sky it's only a matter of time before we're soaked all over again.

"There you are!"

I turn to see Leo's best friend, Pete, approach us.

"Your costume should be illegal. It's a fire hazard," Pete continues, poking at the squashed front of Leo's costume. "But then, I wouldn't get to laugh at how ridiculous you look."

"Come now," Leo says, "I think I look dashing. Don't you agree, Marie?"

I'm so startled at my inclusion in the conversation that I can't think of a clever reply, so I offer a feeble nod.

"See?" Leo says to Pete. "Anyway, what happened?"

Pete shrugs. "No one knows for sure yet, but the fire department's on its way."

"Do you think they'll cancel the play?" Leo asks.

"Cancel the play?" I blurt out. Somehow that possibility hadn't even crossed my mind. "They can't cancel it, can they?"

"I guess it depends on how much damage there was," Pete says. "But the set pieces all got drenched, so that alone might put a stop to it."

After a few minutes, the fire department shows up and rushes inside. The rest of us are stuck outside, waiting for the report and hoping none of our stuff was caught in the crossfire. Mrs. Gibson, the director, looks on the verge of a panic attack.

The first few drops fall from the sky as we finally get an update. Apparently someone left a curling iron on and it must have fallen over onto something flammable. They put the fire out, but not before it did quite a bit of damage. There's no way we're going to be performing this play here anytime soon. I feel like Tweedle Dumb to think I could actually have my dream come true. They never do.

By the time everyone's belongings are retrieved and sorted out, we've relocated to the gym to avoid the rain that is now coming down hard. Most people just have some water damage to deal with, but a few had left their things in the fire zone. Of course, I was one of the latter. I stare at my sodden, charred backpack in dismay. Between the fire and the sprinkler system, my clothes, textbooks, and notes might as well not exist for all the good they'll do now. The rest of the cast go to the locker rooms to change out of their costumes, but the clothes in my backpack were all I had with me.

"You might as well just keep the costume," Mikayla says when I ask if she has an extra outfit I can borrow. "I don't think we'll need it anymore."

I guess Lily gets her wish after all. At least one of us will be happy.

I trudge down the sidewalk away from school through the downpour. It doesn't matter much since I'm soaked anyway. A car sidles up to the curb beside me.

"Do you want a lift?" Leo, back in his normal clothes, calls through the open window. Blood heats my face.

"No, thanks," I say. "I'll be fine."

"Really, I insist," he says. "I can't let you walk home in this."

I can't think of a good reason not to, so I climb in the passenger seat.

"Sorry, I'm getting water all over your seat," I say.

"It'll dry," he says and pulls away from the curb. "It's a shame they had to cancel the play. I hate to see all our hard work go to waste."

"Yeah, I was looking forward to it." That's probably the biggest understatement I've ever uttered.

We ride in silence for a moment. Why did he have to offer me a ride today, the day when the best part of my life was literally flushed away? The last thing I want right now is for Leo to think I'm a crybaby. I can feel tears looming behind the surface as it all sinks in and struggle to keep them at bay. I knew the play would be over this week, but not like this.

The rest of the short drive goes by in silence before he turns onto our street. He pulls to a stop in front of my house.

"Thanks for the ride," I say as I reach for the door handle.

"Anytime," he says. Does he really mean that? I'm too afraid to ask so I climb out of the car as quickly as I can to prevent more rain from getting inside and hurry to the front door.

Rehearsal had lasted a while before the fiasco, so it's after ten and Hank is already home, and passed out on the couch. The coffee table features an empty bottle of whiskey in the midst of a few empty beer bottles. I pass through the entranceway into the kitchen, making as little noise as possible. Mom is still there, but now a bruise stains her cheek. I wish I could say I'm surprised, but I'm pretty sure Hank's behavior is the reason she tuned out the rest of the world in the first place.

"Looks like we both had bad days," I say as I start to compile a sandwich. One tear manages to escape, but I brush it away.

"What's wrong?"

I jump. I didn't expect Mom to actually reply. It's so rare these days I almost forgot she could. Her eyes are no longer fixed on the wall, but are watching me.

"What isn't?" I say, swallowing the rising lump in my throat. "The play was just ruined. Hank's clearly been hurting you again. And you're... you're never here."

"I'm here now," she says, pushing herself out of her chair. "And I know how to fix everything."

She steps toward me but I back away. Something is really eerie about her. I don't think it's just because she hasn't acknowledged my presence for ages. There's something wrong with the way she's looking at me, but I can't put my finger on what it is.

"What do you mean?" I ask as I bump into the counter, which prevents me from backing any further. She spreads her arms.

"Don't be afraid. I just meant a hug makes everything better."

She reaches me before I can figure out what to do and wraps me in an embrace. I hesitate, and then tentatively return the gesture. I'm still confused but decide I'm just imagining things and that she really is trying to be helpful. It's been so long since I've gotten a hug from her. It feels nice. Then something hard collides with the back of my head and I slump to the ground.

I look up, but everything is hazy and I can't seem to get anything to come into focus.

"You worthless piece of trash," Hank's voice barks at me. Now I see that he stands beside my mom with a broken bottle in his hand. "Always complaining about everything. Do you have any idea how hard I work to keep this family going?"

I scramble to my feet, bewildered by the sudden turn of events. I hadn't heard Hank come in. He's never tried to kill me before, though I suppose I wouldn't put it past him. He pushes my mother away and lunges toward me, raising his arm to strike again. I stumble back, still trying to get my bearings.

"If you're so ungrateful, maybe you shouldn't even be in this family," he growls as he takes a swing at me. The jagged edge of the bottle comes within an inch of my nose. I turn and bolt out the door, hardly noticing the rain as I look around for a place to go. I spot the woods behind the houses on the other side of the street and take off toward them when I hear Hank stomp after me. I rush past Leo's house and into the line of trees.

The deluge and darkness, not to mention lingering haziness, make it hard to see where I'm going, but I manage to dodge any trees that come into my path. I think I hear my name shouted from nearby, but it's hard to know for sure due to the pouring rain. Mud splashes with every step and stains my stockings.

The sound of someone crashing through foliage becomes clear and I can tell Hank's gaining on me. I didn't know drunks could run this fast. My foot catches on something and I sprawl, face-first, on the ground. I throw a hasty look over my shoulder and see a dark figure looming toward me. I scream.

"Marie, calm down! It's me, Leo." The figure steps into an opening and the moonlight confirms he is not the man I feared he would be. "Are you alright? I saw you running like a ghost was chasing you." He offers me his hand and helps me to my feet.

"I.... I..." I don't want him to know the truth, but Hank could reach us any minute. "It's my stepdad. He attacked me. We have to get out of here before he finds us."

"We can go to my house," Leo suggests. "We'll go around so we don't cross paths with him, and then you can stay there until it's safe. Come on."

He pulls me along after him and we weave through the trees for a while.

"I can't see a thing," he says finally, coming to a stop. "We need to get out of this rain. Let's find a someplace to wait a while. I don't think your stepdad will find us now."

"Okay," I agree. I'm just relieved to have someone with me—especially since that someone happens to be Leo. I feel safer already.

"Over there," he says, pointing to a hill rising out of the ground not far ahead. "I think I see a cave."

We duck through the low opening and leave the rain behind, though the wind still blows it toward us.

"We should be safe here," Leo says. No sooner have the words left his mouth than we hear footsteps running through the woods. The sound echoes around us and I can't tell where it's coming from.

"Let's get out of sight," Leo says, crawling into the blackness beyond the mouth of the cave.

"Leo, wait," I call after him, "we don't know what's back there!"

"It can't be worse than what's out there," he insists and continues forward, disappearing from sight. Not wanting to be left alone, I follow him.

"Look, there's a light over there," Leo says. Sure enough, there's a pinprick of light down the way.

"But that's impossible," I say. "Unless someone lives in here and has a lantern."

"Let's check it out," Leo says.

"I don't know about this," I say.

"Don't you want to know what it is?"

"It could be dangerous."

"It's a light in a cave," Leo counters. "It's not like it's a wild animal or something."

I hear him press on and have to admit to myself that my curiosity is piqued. *Curiouser and curiouser,* I can't help but think. The light grows larger as we get closer, but we still can't tell what's causing it or see anything within it. When we reach it, it is coming from a hole about two feet around. Leo lowers himself all the way to the ground and pushes his head and shoulders through the opening.

"Marie, you must see this!" he cries and pulls the rest of his body through.

I hesitate, but when Hank's voice echoes through the cave, I follow after Leo. I'm not sure what I was expecting, but what lies on the other side is certainly not it.

We're standing on a ledge on the side of a mountain. It appears to be the middle of the day and the skies are crystal clear. A vast landscape spread before us is unlike anything I've ever seen. The ground far below is a swirling mixture of purples, pinks, and dusky oranges, like a sunset. I think they might be flowers, but we're too far away to tell for sure. I look back the way we came and notice the mountainside leaning slightly away and extending up so high that I can no longer see the top.

"What is this place?" I ask.

"I don't know," Leo says, and then adds half-jokingly, "Wonderland?"

It may not be Wonderland, but I can't escape the notion that he's not far off. It certainly looks like we've stepped through a portal into another world. But of course, those don't actually exist. Do they?

Leo walks to the edge and peers down.

"I think there's a path down the mountain," he says. "Care to explore it?"

I look back at the small hole we came through, the hole leading back to my horrible stepfather and ruined dreams, and then back at the sunset scenery below.

"Absolutely."

We head down the steep path carved into the side of the mountain. The ledge had been even higher than I thought. As we near the bottom I see that the colors below us are not flowers, but trees, if you could call them that. They don't seem to have leaves, but rather each of them have colored bark.

We reach the bottom in surprisingly short time. Nothing looks quite like anything I've seen before. We look around in wonder at the trees whose branches seem to sway of their own accord with complete disregard to the breeze. Small birds dart about between them and there is a murmur through the air that I presume to be chirps, but somehow it reminds me more of voices, though I can't make out any words. The ground is made up of some sort of thick purple moss, and not far ahead of us a pink river cut through the midst of the trees.

"I don't think we're in Oregon anymore," Leo says.

"No," I agree.

"Oh, so you do speak," a new voice pipes up. We look for the source but see no one. "But you aren't all that intelligent regardless, poor things," the voice titters at our baffled expressions.

"It's that bug!" Leo says, pointing at one that was hovering a few feet away. "Or... whatever it is."

"By 'bug,' you had better mean 'most wonderful creature in the world,'" the voice says with an indignant tone.

"It's a fairy," I say. That's one sentence I never thought I would say in any context outside of fiction.

"Indeed I am," says the fairy, the wings on its back flapping so fast as to be all but invisible, with a trail of glittering dust falling behind it. "Do all baby giants wear such peculiar outfits?"

"We're not giants," Leo says. "We're humans."

"I told you they weren't giants," another fairy says as it flies up beside the first. "But no, you never listen to me."

"You were the one who said they couldn't talk, and clearly you were wrong about that, so why should I listen to you?" asks the first.

"Humans..." a richer voice says as though testing the sound of it. I follow the gaze of the two fairies to one of the trees, which I now realize isn't a tree at all but some sort of dryad. "Yes, I've heard of humans. They're more common over in Kalda, I believe."

"Please, will you tell us where we are?" Leo asks.

"Poor things don't know where they are," says the first fairy. "Poor unintelligent things."

"You're in Sonara, of course," the dryad says.

"I've never heard of Sonara," Leo says.

"Never heard of—why, it's worse than I thought," the first fairy says in dismay. "You really are a hopeless case."

"Don't mind her," the second fairy says. "Kalda is easy enough for you two to get back to. Just follow that river downstream and you'll be there before you know it."

"But we're not—" Leo starts, but I cut him off.

"Thank you. We should get started before it gets dark."

"Before what gets dark?" the second fairy wonders.

"The day," I say.

"Such silly creatures," the first fairy murmurs.

"Let's go," I say to Leo and head for the river. He follows along.

"Why were you in such a hurry to leave?" he asks. "We were talking to actual fairies and a dryad!"

"I tend not to enjoy conversations in which my intelligence is constantly called into question," I say. "Besides, I want to see more. If there are humans in Kalda, they might be less condescending."

We reach the water and stare at the light pink hue.

"Do you suppose it's safe to drink?" Leo asks.

"I don't know," I say. "If the trees are alive, I'm hesitant to assume the river isn't. Though I would like to wash this mud off." We've dried by now, but I'm covered in mud from my earlier spill.

"Are you alive?" Leo calls out to the rushing water.

A cat's head emerges from the surface and watches us curiously. "Well, I should hope so."

"I thought cats hated water," I say.

"Cats certainly do," says the creature. "Catfish are another matter entirely." It makes a diving motion, and the rest of its body flashes past, revealing a fishtail protruding from the waist instead of hind legs. The head appears again.

"Can we drink the water?" Leo asks.

"I don't know, can you?" the catfish asks.

Leo kneels beside the river's edge and dips his hand in the water. The mud that coats it immediately vanishes without a trace. He scoops some water to his mouth and takes a cautionary sip.

"Mm, this is delicious!" he says. "You should try it, Marie."

It doesn't seem to be causing him any ill effects, though it could be too soon to tell. I wash my hands off and splash some of the water on my face. A few drops land on my lips and I lick them. The flavor is what I would expect roses to taste like. I scoop up a handful and drink it. It's instantly refreshing. Some of the water slips through my fingers onto my muddied apron, returning the spots it hits to pure whiteness. I touch the clean spots and find that they are already dry. I splash more water onto me and soon I'm clean.

"So, what's the catch?" I ask the catfish.

"What do you mean?" it asks.

"We came through a portal to a world full of fairies, dryads, talking animals, and magic water," I say. "There's got to be something wrong. Evil queens, wicked witches, pirates... What is it here?"

"Nothing," the catfish says.

"That's the worst one," I mumble, but I know what it means.

"I beg your pardon?" Leo says.

"I'm not offended," I say automatically. A baffled expression crosses Leo's face.

"I was just quoting the play," I explain, blushing. We had spent so many weeks memorizing the lines, I assumed he would recognize it, but instead I must have sounded silly.

"Ah, yes, of course" he says.

"Sonara has been a land of perfect peace for as long as anyone can remember," the catfish continues. "Just ask the dryads. They've been around the longest."

"Why would you assume there's a

problem?" Leo asks me.

"There's always a problem," I say. "Nothing is ever perfect. Sooner or later something's going to come up."

"What if it doesn't?" Leo asks. "What if we explore this whole land and find no issue with it whatsoever?"

"Then I'd start seriously considering the possibility that I've died and gone to heaven," I scoff.

"I'm serious," Leo says.

"That's never going to happen," I say.

"Why are you so cynical?" he asks.

"Because," I say, lowering my eyes. "I've learned the hard way that happy endings don't exist."

"This morning, I didn't think magical worlds existed either," Leo offers. I stare into his eyes, and he meets my gaze with a hopeful look. But I can't dare to hope. It hurts too much.

"Let's just get to Kalda," I say. "Maybe they'll have something I can change into."

"But your outfit suits you perfectly," Leo says. "Alice found herself in Wonderland,

and you've found yourself in Sonara."

We walk downstream. I hope Kalda isn't far, but if the dryad was only vaguely familiar with humans, and they've been around the longest, then it's probably not close enough for them to cross paths.

"I don't mean to pry, but I've been wondering, why would your stepfather attack you and chase you into the woods?" Leo asks after some time. With all that has happened, I've all but forgotten what brought us here.

"I'm not really sure," I say. "He just freaked out." I realize my head doesn't hurt like it should and reach up to feel where the bottle hit. There isn't even a lump. That water must have healing properties, too. If only water was like this back home.

"How strange that he would do such a thing," Leo says.

"Not really," I say. "I mean, he's never hit me on the head with a bottle before, but—" I cut off suddenly realizing what

I'm saying. Leo stops in his tracks just in front of me, causing me to stop as well, and turns to face me.

"Marie," he says slowly, "does he do this sort of thing often?"

I don't know what to say. "Can we talk about something else?"

"If he's hurting you, you should tell someone."

I step around him and keep walking, but my mind is racing. The first person to figure out the truth just had to be the guy I have a crush on. He catches up to me.

"Is that what you meant when you said there's no happy endings?" he asks.

"Yeah," I say. Well, it's part of it, but I don't want him prying into the real reason.

"But that's not the ending," Leo says. "That's just part of the journey. Maybe this is your happy ending."

"I can't stay here forever," I say.

"Why not?"

Yes, why not? It's not like I was better off back home. I doubt anyone will even notice I'm gone, especially now that the play has been cancelled. Except...

"No," I say, stopping suddenly. "I have to go back! I can't leave my sister by herself! She's too little to take care of herself, and without me..."

"What about your mum?"

"She can't take care of herself, either." I'm not as sympathetic about this as I should be. Lily doesn't have a choice in the matter. "We should go back. I don't know what I was thinking. I can't leave Lily alone in that house."

"So soon?" Leo asks. "Don't you understand what an incredible opportunity this is? We may be the first people ever to find this place, and you want to leave before we get to see anything?"

"We've seen fairies and dryads. It'll have to do. Besides, we know where the entrance is. I can just go back to get Lily and bring her here with me."

"What if you can't get back? What if you can only go through once, or it's only open for a limited time?"

"Then I'm no worse off than I was before I came here, but at least Lily won't be alone. You don't have to come with me if you don't want to."

"No, I'll come," he says with a sigh. "I won't let you go alone."

"You don't have to cross back over," I say. "You can just—"

"Walk you to the door," he finishes. "So to speak."

We turn around and head upstream in silence. Fear starts building inside me as I picture Lily crying while Hank yells at her like he always does to me. He's never hurt her before, but if I'm not there...

"Oh, no," Leo says.

"What?" I ask, breaking out of my thoughts. Then I see it—gray clouds building in the sky ahead of us.

"Another storm?" I moan. "We just got away from one."

"We better hurry," Leo says. "It's still a ways off."

We break into a trot, keeping an eye on the storm as it gets visibly bigger every moment. What if we can't find the mountain trail in the rain? What if I can't get back? What will happen to Lily?

"Marie..."

I almost stumble as I jerk my head toward the voice. A girl's voice. Lily's. It's faint, but I recognize it. I can't see her anywhere.

"Lily?" I cry, searching frantically for her.

"Marie!" The voice is a little clearer now. Just then, the clouds spread over me in a thick fog. It's so dense I can't even see Leo anymore. I stop running for fear of crashing into some unseen obstacle.

"Lily! Leo!"

"Over here!" Leo's voice comes from my left. I head toward it.

"Leo?" I call as I stumble blindly forward.

"Marie, follow my voice," he says. It's much closer than before. In two more steps, he comes into view. And there's someone next to him.

"Marie!" Lily cries in delight and runs

to me, throwing her arms around me. I squeeze her tight, afraid to let go. "Oh, I'm so glad I found you! I got so scared in this fog."

"How did you get here?" I ask.

"I followed you," she says. "But you got so far ahead of me I thought I'd never catch up."

"You have no idea how happy I am that you're here," I say. "I was so worried about you. Now we just need to get out of this storm."

"I, uh, I'm not so sure this is a storm," Leo says.

A sudden gust of wind blows the fog away. I look up and my jaw drops. Not far above us, sunlight glistens off the shiny green scales of a huge dragon. Its wings flap again, creating a wind that nearly knocks us over. I see now that the clouds were actually coming from its mouth. The dragon flies fast, and it's soon well away from us.

"That's so cool!" Lily says.

"Yeah," I say. "But it's a good thing it

didn't see us."

"The catfish said this is a world of peace, so I doubt it would have harmed us even if it had," Leo says.

"Still, better safe than sorry," I say. "This is Lily, my sister. Lily, this is Leo."

"Hi," Lily says.

"Hello," Leo says. He looks to me. "Well, now that she's here, there's no point in heading this way, is there?"

"No, I guess not," I say.

I take Lily's hand and we head back downstream.

"It's so beautiful here!" Lily says, waving to a dryad.

"Yes, it is," I agree, and then remember something. "Lily, you didn't even notice my dress!"

Lily looks me up and down and smiles. "Oh, yes, it's just right."

I smile back. We continue to walk for what feels like forever, Lily constantly pointing out interesting sights and exclaiming over how pretty things are until finally she complains that she is hungry.

"I wonder how much farther it is," I comment as I peer ahead but can see no change in the landscape.

"Why don't we rest for a while," Leo suggests.

We sit down by the river and drink some of the water. I see no food nearby, though I suppose the food here could have a different appearance. But the water reveals another magical feature when we're soon fulfilled. As we drink, Lily picks the flowers that grow in the shallows of the river. She reaches for one just beyond her grasp and loses her balance, falling in with a splash.

"Lily!" I reach for her, but she comes up laughing.

"It's the perfect temperature," she says. "You should try it!"

"No thanks, I'm fine up here," I say.

"Spoilsport," she says and takes a deep breath before going back under.

"Lily, come out of there," I call.

"Let her be," Leo says. "She's having

fun."

"But we don't know what's in there, other than catfish. And what if she gets stuck underwater, or the current pushes her away, or—"

Lily pops back up. "Are you sure you don't want to come in?"

"Lily, please, come out."

Before she can reply, a catfish's head surfaces, and then another and another. They watch Lily curiously.

"Aw, how adorable," Lily says.

One emerges right beside her and nuzzles against her cheek, causing her to giggle.

"You have nothing to worry about," one of them says to me. "The water is perfectly safe. The current's not too strong, but if she does get caught up in it, we'll bring her back."

"See, there's no need to be afraid," Leo says.

"You know, you're putting an awful lot of faith in a creature we know nothing about," I say.

"Have you seen anything to prove otherwise?" Leo asks.

"Well, not yet..."

"Why is it so hard for you to relax and believe that things might not be all bad?"

"That's how things always seem to turn out for me." I watch Lily play with the catfish. As Lily rotates in a circle with her floating hair trailing behind her, a baby catfish popped its head out and chased after it. "I can't risk letting something happen to her. I don't know what I'd do if I lost her, too."

"Too?" Leo asks.

I sigh. I might as well get it out in the open. He already knows more than anyone else, and he seems to be handling it well so far. "I wasn't always like this. I used to be happy, to feel safe."

"What changed?"

I don't answer right away. I've never really told this to anyone.

"My dad left when I was seven."

"I'm so sorry," Leo says, a sympathetic expression creasing his brow. "My parents are divorced, too. Do you at least get to see him sometimes?"

I shake my head. "That's the thing, we don't know where he went. One day he was just ... gone. Not even a note telling us why. I thought he was happy."

"Maybe something happened to him," Leo suggests.

"That's what I thought, too," I say. "I came up with all kinds of possibilities, like he was kidnapped and taken to South America or something. Seven-year-olds have vivid imaginations. We even had the police search for him, but they never found him. Eventually we just had to accept the truth. He'd left us, and he was never coming back. So she got a divorce."

"Is that when your mum starting dating Hank?" Leo asks.

I nod. "She couldn't really take care of us by herself, and I think she just didn't want to be alone, so she got together with the first man that gave her any attention. When she got pregnant with Lily, they got married. And, well, ever since then my life's been pretty much a living hell. The only good thing to come out of all of this was Lily."

"Now it all makes sense," Leo says. "I'm sorry I was so hard on you. I just wanted you to enjoy yourself."

"No, I'm the one who should be apologizing," I say. "I'm being unfair. You were right. Nothing here has been dangerous so far. I'm overreacting."

Leo puts a hand reassuringly on my knee and looks me straight in the eye. "I promise I won't let anything bad happen to her, or to you. I mean that."

I forget to breathe for a moment. I wasn't expecting such a reaction from him. He leans a little closer, and I get the sudden impression he means to kiss me.

"We've rested long enough," I say and drop my gaze, hoping my hair hides the color of my cheeks. "We should get going." I get to my feet. "Lily, it's time to go."

"Fine," she pouts and swims to the edge. Her clothes dry as she climbs out of the river. "Goodbye!" she calls back to the catfish, waving. There are quite a large number of them now. They all roll under the water and stick their tails out, waving back.

I hold out my hand for Lily, and as she takes it I find that my other hand is being grasped as well.

"If it's all right?" Leo says. I swallow hard and nod, and we set out once again for Kalda.

Stupid, stupid, stupid! I condemn myself. Leo was about to kiss me, and I just walked away. What was I thinking? It's what I've wanted for ages. But maybe I misinterpreted it. He was being kind, and I just took that to mean more than it was. Why would he want to kiss me after only like two conversations ever? I replay the scene in my mind. No, that was definitely the expression of someone right before they go in for the kiss. Not that I would know personally, of course, since no one's ever looked at me that way before, but that's how it looks in the movies. Besides, now he's holding my hand. *Oh God, Leo Hughes is holding my hand!*

"It's a shame we never talked much before this," Leo muses. "I wish I had gotten to know you sooner."

"Yeah, same here," I manage to choke out and hope my voice sounds natural.

"I'd actually been meaning to talk to you more, but, well, I could never quite get the nerve up."

"What do you mean?"

Leo glances down, suddenly embarrassed. "You see, I ... I've actually fancied you for a while now."

My heart stops. Lily gasps in delight and giggles.

"I never realized," I say.

"I hope I haven't alarmed you," he says, looking up with concern. "If you don't feel the same —"

"No," I cut him off, meeting his hazel eyes again. "Actually, I do."

His face breaks into the most marvelous smile I've ever seen.

"Leo and Marie, sitting in a tree..." Lily sings. For a split second I think I see Leo's smile falter, a strange look flashing across his eyes, but then it's gone and I question whether I was imagining it. I can never let myself trust that anything is good, so I'm probably making up anything to prove this is some sort of joke. I look away as the thought sinks in. What if this is a joke? What if he was only messing with me, and now I admitted my feelings for him?

We continue on in silence for some time, each moment getting more awkward than the last, but none of us venture to break it. I can only imagine what Leo might be thinking right now. I glance toward him, but he's staring straight ahead with a blank expression. I suddenly realize how odd it is that Lily hasn't been filling the silence, either, and turn to her. She, too, is wearing a blank expression.

"Guys?" I say, beginning to feel uneasy. Neither reacts. Then I notice it, a gentle chorus of voices singing in the distance. I don't know how I didn't notice it before, but now that I'm aware of it, I think I remember it building in the background. It seems to be a sort of wordless melody, and it is easily the most beautiful song I've ever heard. It grows louder the further we walk, and I become less and less aware of anything else.

We turn a bend, and I finally see the source. Three beautiful women stand ankle deep in the river on the opposite side of it. They are all reaching up to the sky, their eyes closed as they harmonize. At once, all of them open their eyes and look in our direction. They lower their arms until they appear to be beckoning us toward them.

Splash. With a jolt, I realize I've stepped into the river. Lily, too, looks around as though surprised, but I feel Leo's hand slip out of mine.

"Leo, wait!" I cry, but he's already waist deep. Understanding fills me with horror. *Sirens.* "Leo, it's a trap! Come back."

But Leo doesn't slow, now deep enough to swim. I hurry after him and snatch his shirt when I'm close enough. His head snaps back toward me with a terrifying glower.

"Leave me alone," he snarls. I'm so stunned I let go. "Why would I want you when I could have them?"

With that he turns back to the sirens and finishes crossing the river. I watch numbly as two of them take his hands in theirs and they all walk away from the river, past the line of dryads, and out of sight. I float in the river for a moment, too shocked to know what else to do. He was right, of course. I'm nothing compared to their beauty. Why should he choose me? I just thought maybe, just this once, I could actually trust someone.

"Marie!" Lily's shout startles me and I'm suddenly aware that the current has been pushing me away from her. She runs along the bank after me, but the current moves faster every second.

The sirens' song has faded, and a new sound replaces it, a rumbling sound that I realize is an approaching waterfall. I begin swimming toward Lily's side of the river, but the current is so strong now that I don't seem to be making any progress. Suddenly, the water below me surges upward, lifting me with it, and carries me safely to the opposite bank. As the water disappears into the ground, I find myself completely dry.

"Are you well?"

I raise my eyes to see the most handsome man I've ever laid eyes on. His dark, wavy hair contrasts with his bright blue eyes, which crinkle in concern as he approaches me. His white shirt is tucked into his black leather pants, ending in a pair of black boots. He's every bit Prince Charming.

"I, uh, I think so," I stammer. "How did you do that?"

"I'm on good terms with the naiads," he says.

I look back across the river to where

Lily stands, watching us.

"My sister..."

A sudden gust of wind picks her up and carries her across, setting her down gently on our side.

"And how did you do *that?*" I ask as I get to my feet.

"I'm also on good terms with the aurae," he says. "My name is Sebastian."

"I'm Marie," I say.

"I'm Lily," my sister pipes up before I have the chance to introduce her.

"What were you doing in the river so close to the fall?" Sebastian asks.

Oh, nothing, just chasing after my first shot at love.

"She was trying to save her boyfriend from the sirens," Lily answers for me.

"Lily!" I can imagine the shade of red my cheeks are now. This seems to be happening far too often lately. "He isn't my boyfriend."

"Sirens," Sebastian says, giving me a sympathetic look. "They can capture the hearts of the greatest men."

"What brings you all the way out here?" I ask, grasping for a change in subject. "Or, are we finally close to Kalda?"

"Kalda is still a ways off," he says.

So much for 'You'll be there before you know it.' That's the last time I trust a fairy for directions.

"I was just on my way back there from Periat. Is that where you are going?"

"Yes," I say.

"Then why don't we go together?" Sebastian asks.

"Can you teach us how to do that thing you did with the water and the wind?" Lily asks.

"Well, I suppose that depends on how well you get along with the nymphs," Sebastian says, "but I could introduce you to them."

"I don't know, I think we should just go on our own," I say. After what happened with Leo, I'm in no mood to trust a complete stranger.

"But he saved your life!" Lily says.

"We can't just walk away. Besides, we're heading the same way anyway." She has a point.

I sigh. "Fine. But you don't have to introduce us to the nymphs," I say to Sebastian.

"Aw, why not?" Lily asks.

"You're too young to mess with elemental stuff," I reply.

"They wouldn't follow any dangerous requests," Sebastian says. "Here, let me call them for you."

He kneels down and puts one hand on the ground, murmuring something too softly for me to make out. Here and there, the mossy ground rises up into small, fluffy beings. It reminds me of gophers popping out of the ground.

"These are limoniads," Sebastian says.

"Lemonades?" Lily asks, furrowing her brow. There's no way that's what they're called.

"Li-*mown*-ee-ads," Sebastian emphasizes and reaches a hand out to one. It touches the ground, which surges at its touch, and in a moment it holds up a small mossy wreath and gives it to Sebastian. He takes it and places it atop Lily's head. Lily applauds with glee.

"This is Marie and Lily," Sebastian says to the limoniads, "sisters of... Where did you say you were from?"

"We didn't," I say. "Nowhere you'd know of."

"I know all of the lands," Sebastian says.

"Well, we're not exactly from these lands," I say.

"Did you come through a portal?" Sebastian says, raising his eyebrows.

"Yeah, you know about those?" I ask.

"A good friend of mine came through one a long time ago," Sebastian says. "He tried to find a way back, but never could track one down. He would be so happy to learn that someone else has come through one—do you think you could show him the way back?"

"I guess, but he might not even be from the same place as us," I say.

"He said it was someplace called... let

me think... Ore-gin," Sebastian says.

"Oregon?" I say. Something tickles the back of my mind, but I ignore it. "That's where we're from."

"Perfect!" Sebastian says. "If you wouldn't mind helping him out, I know he would be incredibly grateful. He just wants to get back to his family."

The tickling grows, but the likelihood is far too slim to give serious consideration.

"Anyway, these are the nymphs of the meadow," Sebastian redirects us back to the original topic.

"Hello," Lily says. "And thank you for the wreath."

"You're welcome," the one that made it says to her.

"Can you make one for my sister?" Lily asks. The limoniad repeats the movement and holds a second wreath out to me.

"Thank you," I say as I take it and position it to match Lily's.

"Then there are the water nymphs, the naiads," Sebastian says, pointing back toward the river. We follow his finger and see that the water's surface has risen up in places to form liquid silhouettes with undefined features, save two glowing eyes.

"So, the river *is* alive?" I say, thinking back to how much water I drank.

"Not exactly," Sebastian says. "It's more like they reside within the water, so removing some water isn't harmful to them."

Lily waves to them, and they wave back before melting into the river.

"The aurae—those are the wind nymphs—are invisible," Sebastian says, "but they are all around here."

"Hi," Lily says, peering up at the sky.

"I'll introduce you to the mountain nymphs and fire nymphs whenever we come across them. And of course you've already met the dryads."

I frown. "How do you know about that?"

"I'm sorry, I assumed you had because you've been walking near them, and they are the most obvious," he says.

"Oh, right," I say.

"Anyway, whenever you need help from any of them, call to them and ask. Just don't do anything to upset them or they might not listen."

"Can the dryads grow fruit?" I ask. "We haven't eaten since we got here."

"Of course," Sebastian says. "Why don't you try it?"

"Um, okay," I say. I walk up to the nearest dryad. "Hello."

"Hi," it says in a shy voice.

"Would it be possible to get an apple?" I ask.

"Apple?" it replies. "What is that?"

"It's a fruit," I say, my heart sinking. Surely they can't make something they've never heard of.

"I don't know of apples, but I could give you a kremmon," it says. One of the branches moves toward me, and a round, purple fruit grows on the tip to the size of a cantaloupe. It breaks off, and I manage to catch it before it hits the ground.

"Thank you," I say. I bring the

kremmon back to Lily and Sebastian. "How do you eat it?"

"Just bite into it," Sebastian says.

I do so. It tastes similar to an apple with a hint of vanilla. I give it to Lily, who takes a bite.

"So you see, it's pretty simple, as long as you stay friendly with them," Sebastian says.

"I could get used to this," Lily says, and I have to admit I could as well.

When we reach the town of Kalda, Sebastian guides us to his friend's house.

"How long did you say he's been here?" I ask.

"I couldn't say for sure, but it must have been ages," Sebastian says. "It's just up here."

We approach the door of what might be considered a cottage. The houses here are all different shapes and sizes. This one is prism-shaped with triangular windows and doors. Sebastian knocks, and after a moment it opens. For a minute I can only stare in shock.

"Charles, I met some more people from Oregon," Sebastian says, oblivious to my surprise.

Charles...

Charles raises his eyebrows and looks first at Lily, then at me. Then stiffens. I can tell by the look on his face that he's calculating, trying to figure out if I could be the person he thinks I am, but too afraid to say so in case I'm not.

"Dad?" I somehow manage to croak and his eyes go wide.

"Marie?" he asks. I nod. The next thing I know, we're embracing. "Marie, I'm so sorry. I've been trying to get back home for so long, but I couldn't find the way."

"Really?" I ask, clutching him tighter. "I thought... I thought you'd abandoned us."

He releases me and puts his hands on my shoulders, looking me straight in the eye.

"I would never do that."

I feel like a weight that has been pressing

me into the ground for almost a decade has suddenly disappeared. He didn't abandon me. He just couldn't find his way back. And he has been trying to get back to us this whole time. I always hoped I was wrong.

"How's your mother?" he asks, and the joyous feeling dims.

"Uh, not good," I say. "She... she really let herself go when you disappeared."

Dad's eyes fill with sorrow. "I never should have looked in that cave."

"Cave?" I say. "But that's how I got here. What stopped you from going back?"

"I tried, but the entrance in the mountainside was gone. But if it was open today for you to come through, maybe it will still be open if we go back there."

"Or we could just stay here," Lily says. "I mean, wasn't Marie the reason you wanted to go back?"

"That's Lily," I explain to him, "my sister."

His expression changes to shock, and I suddenly realize what he inferred from that. I'm so used to telling everyone she's my sister that I didn't think about what that would mean to my dad.

"So Julia... " he starts, but can't bring himself to finish. I nod frowning with sympathy.

"I'm sorry, but she couldn't take care of me by herself," I say. "She thought you were never coming back."

Dad sighs. "That's understandable. I guess there's no point in looking for a way back, then, if she's found someone else."

My mom's vacant face flashes to my mind, and I wonder if she'd snap out of it if Dad came back. But that would mean we'd have to leave here, and if the entrance is only open at certain times, we may never be able to come back. On the other hand, we'd have my dad, so we could get away from Hank. I guess it isn't really fair to leave her there, even if it was her choice to withdraw from us instead of finding a way to protect us from Hank.

"We should probably at least check it

out. If it's closed, then we'll just stay here, but if it's open, we'll get Mom and try to come back." Maybe she'll revive when she sees this place.

"What if she chooses him over me?" Dad asks.

"I can guarantee you that won't be an issue," I say. He smiles at that.

"We should celebrate our reunion," Dad says. "Come on in. Let's have a feast."

The interior of the cottage appears larger than I expected based on the outside. A long table stretches the length of the room, and Dad swiftly moves to fill it with all kinds of unrecognizable foods. A fire danced in the fireplace, but I realize that it is actually a figure made of fire standing in the middle of it.

"Is that a nymph?" I ask Sebastian. He nods.

"It's called a lampad," he says.

After a few minutes, the table is set, and we all sit down to eat. Everything I try tastes incredible.

"What have you been up to since I

left?" Dad asks me.

"Normal stuff," I say. "School, mostly. I was supposed to be the lead in a play, but then it got cancelled."

"The lead, wow," he says. "That's great, honey. I'm sorry it got cancelled, though. Maybe we can put on a play here sometime. The people here love to act."

"Is there a theater in town?" I ask, intrigued.

"The finest I've ever been to," he says. "Here, try this."

He holds out a bowl of small half-circular yellow fruit. I grab one and take a bite, and Lily does the same. It reminds me of my favorite.

"Mm, this tastes just like strawberries!" Lily says with a smile. I freeze. Lily hates strawberries. With a passion. It's something we argue about frequently — all in fun, of course — because I love them so much. Why would she like them now? I stare at her for a moment, trying to work it out in my head.

Maybe it's no big deal. After all, kids

change their taste preferences all the time. But what bothers me most is the fact that she didn't even blink an eye when she said it. It just isn't like Lily at all. Besides, just this morning she—morning?

We had entered the cave at nighttime in our world, and had walked a long time before we reached Kalda, but it was still light out here. I try to think back to how low the sun was in the sky when we came inside, but I can't seem to remember seeing a sun at all here. I don't feel tired, despite it probably being somewhere early morning back home. Maybe the water or food is keeping us energized longer than normal, but it's way past Lily's bedtime. This thought process has nothing to do with whether or not Lily likes strawberries, and there's probably some explanation for it in this crazy world, but in light of Lily's sudden change it just feels somehow wrong.

"Come to think of it, I believe there's a play performing today," Dad says, breaking my chain of thought. "If you'd like, we can go after we finish eating."

"We have to go back and get Mom," I say.

"Can't we do that after?" Lily asks. "I wanna see the play!"

"You heard what my dad said. The way back might be closed by then."

"It's probably closed already," Lily says. "Let's just stay here."

"Lily, don't you want Mom to be here, too?" I ask. Lily has always cared a lot more about our mom than I have. She still talks to her as though she's listening and shows her pictures she draws as though she sees. First she likes strawberries, and now she wants to ditch our mom to live alone with Hank when I'm the one fighting for her? What's going on? It's almost as if —

"I'm sure what Lily's trying to say is that you've walked so far already, and it would be good to rest for a while," Sebastian says.

"Yes, of course that's what I meant," Lily says. "We'll go back tomorrow after we've rested."

"If tomorrow ever comes," I mutter.

"What was that?" Sebastian asks with a frown.

"Well, it doesn't seem to be getting dark around here, and the fairies called me silly for saying that it would."

"Fairies have their own light," Sebastian explains. "Nothing seems dark to them."

"Uh-huh," I say, but my mind has gone back to the issue of Lily. "Lily, how did you say you found us?"

"I followed you," she says.

"I didn't see you in the house," I say.

"I was in my room. I came out when I heard something."

"You must have been pretty fast to catch up to me before Hank did," I say.

"Maybe he went the wrong way," Lily suggested.

"Does all this really matter?" Sebastian asks. "She's here now. That's what's important. She's safe from Hank."

My eyes snap to him. "I never told you

anything about Hank."

"But you just said—"

"I said she reached me before Hank did, but that doesn't necessarily mean Hank put me in danger."

"I'm sorry, I just assumed—"

"You do a lot of that, don't you?" I say. "Who are you, anyway? You just happen to show up when I'm about to drown, happen to know my dad, and now you're speaking for my sister. I don't even know you!"

"Marie, please, just calm down," he says. "Is it really so strange that I would help a girl in trouble, or recall the one person I've met who has come from another land? I was just trying to help."

"Well, maybe I don't need your help," I say, getting to my feet. "Lily, Dad, let's go. Maybe the aurae can give us a ride back to the entrance."

Then the strangest thing happens. Dad and Lily both look to Sebastian, as if seeking his approval in the plan. I follow their gaze and catch him giving them a meaningful look, though the meaning is lost on me, before he wipes it from his face when he realizes I'm looking.

"What's going on?" I ask. Now I'm more convinced than ever that something weird is happening.

"What do you mean?" Lily asks, but her voice sounds too casual.

"You magically appear right when I go looking for you, Sebastian shows up out of the blue and leads us right to my long-lost father, everyone keeps trying to convince me to stay here and not even try to go back, and now you're both looking to Sebastian as though he gets the final say? And Lily hates strawberries! Somebody had better tell me what is going on right now."

"We have to tell her," Lily says in a quiet voice to Sebastian, which earns her a heated glare from him. My heart skips a beat. I was right. I don't think I actually expected that. But how can Lily be involved in whatever this is? Is it even really her?

"Tell me what?" I press. No one speaks for a moment. Finally Sebastian heaves a sigh.

"I suppose it's for the best, now that you are aware. I had hoped you wouldn't notice."

"How could I not notice my sister isn't herself?"

"That wasn't part of the original plan," Sebastian says, but you have a hard time letting things go."

"What plan?" I ask. Now I'm getting really concerned.

"The plan to make you happy," Sebastian says. That's not what I expected to hear.

"What do you mean?" I ask.

"You're always so unhappy," Sebastian says. "I hate to see you that way. I wanted you to be happy, and safe."

And now I'm mainly creeped out. "I've never met you before. How would you know whether or not I'm happy?"

"You never saw me, but I've been watching you for a long time," Sebastian says. "When the play was ruined, I couldn't handle seeing you so upset anymore. It was time to act. So I brought you here."

"You weren't even there," I say, backing away from the table.

"I was in charge of everything."

I'm suddenly aware that the room is dimmer and the food and table are gone.

"What is this place?" I ask.

"It's where all your dreams can come true," Sebastian says. "For it is the land of dreams."

"The land of dreams?" I repeat in confusion.

"When humans sleep, their souls leave their bodies and enter a spirit realm. Humans call them 'dreams' because they do not understand the truth. In typical sleep, a soul remains strongly linked with the body, able to reenter it at a moment's notice if need be, but the further a soul travels into the realm, the more real it becomes. Everything here can be influenced by you. You can have anything you want, anything you can dream of."

"I'm asleep?" I ask.

"I've been calling to you in your dreams for a while now. You just never strayed far enough from your body to be able to stay here. But now you can."

I don't understand," I say. "If this is all just a dream, aren't you something I made up? How could you watch me and call to me?"

"The settings are fabricated," Sebastian says. "They can be anything."

I look around and see that the house has disappeared and we are now standing on what appears to be thin air. All around us is darkness dotted with stars, as though we are in outer space.

"The people, though; we are real. Or rather, we aren't your creation, though we are not technically people. We are beings of this realm, and as such we change to fit your needs and desires. You wanted your sister, and so one of us who happened to be nearby became her."

"And let me guess," I break in. "I wanted my father to be here, so someone became him, too?"

Sebastian nods.

"So he was never really here. He really did abandon me."

"Wouldn't you prefer a world in which he didn't?" Sebastian asks, stepping toward me. I take a step back. "Wouldn't you rather be in a place where you make the rules? Where you decide who's there and who isn't, and how they treat you?"

"But it's not real!" I say. "I'll still know that it's just a copy of them, that they're still out there—" I break off, realizing. "Lily's still back there! I left her all alone! I have to go back!"

"Marie, please, listen to me!"

"No! My sister needs me. That's real. And I demand to know how to get out of here."

"Marie."

Lily's voice, faint and distorted, reaches me from above. Before I truly comprehend what I'm doing, I launch through the air toward it.

"Marie, wait!" Sebastian's voice calls

from behind, but I ignore him.

I don't question how I'm doing what I'm doing as I rocket toward the source of Lily's voice. The stars around me fade and a white light appears ahead of me. It takes the form of a white room, and now I see the truth.

My body is lying in a bed with closed eyes. I watch from above. I spot Lily sitting on the chair beside me, grasping my hand. There are some cables connecting my body to contraptions, and I realize I'm in a hospital.

"They found a different place to do the play," Lily tells my body. "If you just wake up, then you can be Alice." She takes a deep, shaky breath and I realize how frightened she is. "Please wake up, Marie. Why won't you wake up?"

I push forward, aiming for my body, but just before I reach it I see Sebastian flash past me and crash into it first. As he does, he is seemingly absorbed into my body. My body opens her eyes.

"Lily?" my body says, but it's not me.

It's him controlling me, I know it.

"Lily, get away from him!" I cry, but she can't hear me.

"Marie!" she says in excited disbelief. I reach for my body, but something prevents me from touching it. I can only watch in horror as Sebastian, in my body, pulls her into a hug.

"I knew you'd wake up! I just knew it!" Lily says, burying her head in my hair. Sebastian reaches one of my arms out, grabs the rod holding up the IV bag, and slams it down hard on her head. Lily crumples to the floor, a red stain now marring her blonde hair.

"No!" I scream as Sebastian emerges from my body, which also slumps down unconscious. "What did you do?!"

"Now you have no reason to leave," he says, his voice as calm as it was when he explained the peculiar truth of this world.

I turn and speed away to the left. All I can think to do is get as far away from him as possible.

"Marie, come back!" Sebastian cries. I

don't have to look back to know he's right behind me.

What looks like a wall made of gel comes into view in front of me but I hit it before I can change course. A ripple shivers through me at the touch, and suddenly I'm somewhere else. Surprise brings me to a stop as I look around.

I'm in a house I've never seen before. A teenage guy and a girl I don't recognize stand in the living room, looking out a window.

"We can't let the water inside," the boy says. Something hits my shoulder and I look up to see ice cubes raining from the ceiling. I look back to the couple, and the girl now has a crossbow in her hand. I get the distinct impression that I've somehow stepped into her dream. She sees me and aims the bow at me.

I take off to the nearest door, but when I open it water crashes over me. After a moment of panic, I remember this is a dream and find that I don't have to breathe. I swim around, looking for a way out, when I see Sebastian swimming toward me. I take off in the opposite direction. Another gel wall is ahead, and I swim to it as fast as I can.

I find myself standing on a sidewalk behind three people.

"What's that?" one of them asks, pointing.

As I try to look at the thing skittering around on the floor, I can never seem to see it clearly. At first I think it's an ant, but then it seems to be a spider. I realize it's larger than that, closer to a scorpion or centipede. By the time I'm finally able to look straight at it, it's grown so much that it has become a snake. It lets out a growl and springs at the group of people. I turn down an alley and head for another gel wall at the end.

I'm in a hospital, but not the one my body was in. Tons of injured people are in the waiting room, all calling out for help. A doctor looks overwhelmed by the vast number of them. I run down the hall away from them, but as I pass the doctor I see him pull a gun from under his lab coat. I don't stop. At the end of the hall, I turn and see another familiar wall.

This time I know where I am. It's the school auditorium, and Leo is on stage.

I'm so grateful to see a familiar face that I forget what he said to me when he left. "I need your help."

"Hello, Alice," he says. I look down and remember I'm still wearing my costume.

"No, I'm not Alice, I'm—"

That's when I see him. Pete is approaching Leo, only he's not wearing a shirt. Leo obviously forgets about me right away when he sees him. And based on the look on his face...

I take off once more, looking desperately for another wall. I'm such an idiot. How did I not catch this? But... how could I? He told me he had a crush on me. Only—

I come to a stop just before the wall. Only that was in Sonara. I'd assumed Leo at least had been real, since he crossed through the portal with me, but now that

I stop to think about it that doesn't make sense. How could I have brought another person with me? So even that had been fake. Somehow it hurts more knowing that he never even gave me a second thought than if he'd left me for the sirens. At least then I believed he liked me, even if it had only been until something better came along.

I take a determined step through the wall and somehow I'm not surprised by what I find there. Sebastian is waiting for me. We're in my kitchen, and my mom stands on his left, Lily on his right.

"It was you, wasn't it?" I ask. "You were Leo. That's why you appeared as Sebastian so soon after he left."

Sebastian nodded. "I knew you liked him. I wanted to be the one to give you the happy ending you wished for."

"I don't understand," I say. "Why did you have the sirens steal him away, only to appear in a different form?"

"I'm afraid I became jealous," Sebastian says. "I've been in love with you for so long. I just wanted you to love me, too."

"But he *was* you," I say.

"You didn't know that. I didn't want to spend the rest of our lives with you only loving me because you thought I was him. I wanted you to love me for me."

"Do you even have a form of your own?" I ask. "Is Sebastian even your real name?"

Sebastian looks down but doesn't say anything. That's answer enough.

"I could never love you. Everything you gave me was a lie."

"But it was for your best," Sebastian says, peering up at me with an earnest expression. "I was trying to help you."

"Then you should have left me alone!" I say. "I had my family. That was all I really needed."

"And you can have them now," Sebastian says, gesturing to my mom and sister.

"No!" I say, anger building inside me. "My sister is dead. I watched you kill her. I won't live forever with these shams in their places. This is my dream, and I can do whatever I want. And what I want is for you and all of your fakes to leave me alone!"

As I say these last words, the rage inside me turns into a surge of energy. I release it in their direction, despite Sebastian's attempt to speak up. I don't want to hear another word from him. The energy wave crashes into the three of them and they fall to the floor.

Sebastian sits up without a scratch.

"Do you have any idea what you've done?" he cries.

"Yes," I say. "I took control."

"No, you don't understand! Those weren't spirit versions of them, and this isn't your dream! This is Julia's!"

"Mom's?" I ask, my heart dropping, though I suppose it's just the impression of my heart since I'm not in my body. The world around us dims.

"Hurry!" Sebastian says as he leaps to his feet and runs to me. He grabs my arm and pulls me back through the gel wall before I have a chance to resist. I take one last look over my shoulder and see the world dissipating behind us as we cross through the wall.

"What just happened?" I ask.

"You hit Julia's spirit with that energy. Human spirits can't stand against a force like that. She was dying, and we had to get out before her portion of the spirit realm collapsed.

"Dying? But—"

"Don't you get it?" Sebastian yells in my face. "I didn't kill Lily. I knocked her out so I could bring her spirit here, so she would be safe, just like I did to you when I took over your mother's body and hit you on the head."

"Hank hit me on the head," I counter.

"No, you just imagined that as a way of reconciling the facts," Sebastian says. "You couldn't believe your mother would do it, but Hank would. You've been in a dream since that moment."

"But my mom—"

"She's been sending her spirit here for

ages, even while she's awake. She's the one who asked me to look over you, the reason I watched you until I fell in love and decided to bring you here."

My mind spun with the information.

"But then, if that was really Mom and Lily..."

Sebastian gives me a sorrowful look.

"What happens when a spirit is destroyed within the realm?"

"This is the realm of spirits," Sebastian says. "If they are destroyed inside here, then... then they are destroyed completely."

Everything inside me goes numb. This isn't possible...

~*~

My eyes open. I'm in the hospital bed.

"Marie!" Lily cries. "I knew you'd wake up! I just knew it!"

"Lily!" I say in relief and pull her into a hug. She buries her head in my hair.

"Guess who else woke up?" she asks

excitedly as she pulls back. I turn to see my mom smiling at us, that wonderful smile I haven't seen in years, joyful tears filling her eyes.

"I'm so sorry I was away," she says. "I'll never leave you again."

"Neither will I," another voice says. Leo is standing beside her. I smile and open my arms to receive them all in one big hug.

~*The End*~

We hope you enjoyed reading *A World of My Own* by Becca Bates. Please consider visiting your favorite online venue to post a review!

To find more exciting and engaging books, please visit Indie Artist Press at ***www.indieartistpress.com***.

About the Author

Becca Bates was born in August 1990 in southern California. From an early age, she was an avid reader and often created stories of her own, though it wasn't until high school that she began writing her first novel.

After writing for a few years as a side hobby, her love for it grew until she decided it was her greatest passion and something worth pursuing professionally.

A World of My Own is her first professional publication, and she is currently working on a full-length fantasy series called *The Eridan Chronicles*.

She makes her home in Fort Collins, Colorado.

You can contact Becca at:

http://beccabates.weebly.com

www.ingramcontent.com/pod-product-compliance
Lightning Source LLC
Chambersburg PA
CBHW020534120726
47904CB00003B/1072